Discard

The Three Goats

Modern Curriculum Press
BEGINNING
TO
READ
Series

Copyright © 1963 by Modern Curriculum Press. Original copyright © 1963 by
Follett Publishing Company. All rights reserved. Printed in the United States
of America. This book or parts thereof may not be reproduced in any form or
mechanically stored in any retrieval system without written permission of the
publisher.
Library of Congress Catalog Card Number: 63-9616

ISBN 0-8136-5554-4 (Paperback)
ISBN 0-8136-5054-2 (Hardcover)

7   8   9   10   92

The Three Goats

Margaret Hillert

illustrated by Mel Pekarsky

MODERN CURRICULUM PRESS
Cleveland · Toronto

6

See the goats.

One, two, three goats.

Goats can run and jump.

The little goat said, "I want something.

I want to find something.

Away I go."

8

See the goat go.

The little goat can go up.

Up, up, up.

Look down here.

Here is something funny.

Run, run, run.

Jump, jump, jump.

Here I go.

Little goat, you can not go.

I want you, little goat.

Here I come.

Not I, not I.

Oh, help, help.

Away I go.

Jump, jump, jump.

Oh my, oh my.

See the little goat run away.

Here I come.

I want something.

I can come up here.

Goat, goat.

Come down.

Come down to me.

I want you.

Not I, not I.

I can run away.

Run, run, run.

And jump, jump, jump.

Oh my, oh my.

The goat can run and jump.

The goat can run away.

Big goat wants something.

See the big, big goat.

20

Here I come.

Here I come.

I see you, big goat.

I want you.

Come down here.

Not I.

You can not make me come down.

Come up here to me.

Look, big goat, look.

Here I come for you.

And—

Here you go!

Down.

Down.

Down.

See here.

See here.

We can run.

We can jump.

We can play.

We can run and play.

Margaret Hillert, author and poet, has written many books for young readers. She is a former first-grade teacher and lives in Birmingham, Michigan.

The Three Goats

Attractive and amusing pictures of the old story of the Billy Goats Gruff, with a text that uses 36 preprimer words.

Word List

7	see		want	**13**	you
	the		something		not
	goats		to		come
	one		find		
	two		away	**14**	oh
	three		go		help
	can	**9**	up	**15**	my
	run				
	and			**17**	me
	jump	**10**	look		
			down	**20**	big
			here		
				23	make
8	little				
	said		is	**24**	for
	I		funny	**27**	play